WOMEN AND THE SEA and Ruth!

written and illustrated by Richard J. King
with additional text by Elysa R. Engelman

Ruth ran to the museum when she heard about the new exhibit. She heard that the museum had stories and paintings and photographs and fishing gear and ship models and wood carvings and clothing and displays of all sorts of things about women and the sea.

Ruth ran to the ticket seller and said, "I, along with my stuffed shark Roy, love the sea!"

"Really?" said the ticket seller, putting down her book.

"Yes," said Ruth. "And we want to know all the ways women, like me, have been on and beside and under the sea."

"You have come to the right place. And your shark goes for free," said the ticket seller. "Go to the building I circled on this museum map."

"Thank you," said Ruth.

Ruth ran to the building circled on the map.

She opened the door, and learned that women
go to sea for...

fun and sport!

Four girls (and one banjo-ukulele) sailing *Aquilo*, 1925

Dawn Riley at age 4

Bumper sticker

Dawn Riley, 1995 captain of the
America's Cup women's team

She learned of women pirates,

The "Jolly Rachel"

Pirates Anne Bonny and Mary Read

POLLY ♀

and of women scientists on oceanography boats.

Rachel Carson, naturalist
and author

BERNICE

Cindy Lee Van Dover,
oceanographer
and *Alvin* pilot

Rock collected from the ocean floor
(9,000 feet under water) by Lisa
Gilbert aboard *Alvin*

She learned of women lighthouse keepers and women aboard ship as doctors and nurses.

A nurse tends an injured sailor

The Civil War hospital ship *Red Rover* carried nurses

Sharon Daley provides medical care to Maine islanders

Lighthouse keeper Ida Lewis, who rescued many shipwrecked men

She learned of women saving lives with the Coast Guard,

A rescue at sea

14

World War II poster
for the Coast Guard
SPARS

Petty Officer 3rd Class
Terry-Ann Gregory
at her station

Lt. Sandra Stoce, first female commanding
officer of a large icebreaking tug

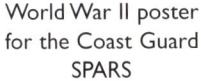

of women fighting in
their country's navies,

Hannah Snell dressed as a
man to join the British Navy

World War II poster
for the Navy WAVES

Kathleen McGrath, commander of the
USS *Jarrett*

Figurehead of a woman warrior

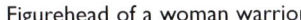

and of women leaving the shore to go fishing!

Eel-Spearing at Setauket by William Sydney Mount, 1845

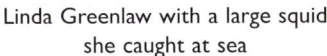
Linda Greenlaw with a large squid she caught at sea

Greenlaw captained this Gloucester swordfishing boat for 4 years

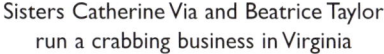
Sisters Catherine Via and Beatrice Taylor run a crabbing business in Virginia

She learned of sea-going mothers, wives, authors, and teachers.

Mary Brewster, who went to Hawaii on a whaleship in 1845

Sue Howell, an astronomy instructor, wife, and mother who was lost at sea in 1984

Mary K. Bercaw Edwards on the
Charles W. Morgan

MOBY-CHICK

She learned of one woman who guided a sailing ship around stormy Cape Horn,

Mary Patten navigating *Neptune's Car* in 1856

and she learned of women working on ships training sailors.

Girl scouts learning to sail a schooner, 1930s

Sail-training vessel *Exy Johnson*, named for a famous female sailor and teacher

Jennifer L. Yount (far left) and her California Maritime Academy cadets

Jen Irving teaching a student how to steer by the wind

At the end of the exhibit, Ruth saw one last set of pictures. She said,
   "Well, these women keep on adaptin'! No matter what boat, some woman's been captain!"
   Ruth and Roy waved goodbye to the exhibit for the day.

Riverboat captain Mary "Ma" Greene

Thea Foss, who started a boat-rental company in the 1880s

STEAMBOAT

MV CONTAINER SHIP

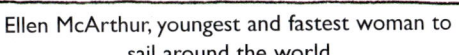
Ellen McArthur, youngest and fastest woman to sail around the world

Michele Gladwin, captain of an 1,100-foot containership

"That is one fine museum," Ruth said to Roy. "I learned that women, like me, have always been on, around, and even under the sea. Women have just had different roles, Roy, changing with the times."

"And you know what else? I love the sea. And she's for me!"

Dawn Riley has been sailing since she was very young. At age 13, she sailed with her family from Detroit to New York and then to the Caribbean. Dawn became captain of the first all-women America's Cup team aboard the *America³* in 1995.

Anne Bonny and **Mary Read** were Englishwomen who dressed as men and joined a pirate crew in the Caribbean. They were captured by authorities in 1720.

Rachel Carson (1907-1964) was a scientist who wrote three best-selling books that together formed what she called a "biography of the sea." She became famous for her warnings about the harmful effects of chemicals on the environment.

Cindy Lee Van Dover is an oceanographer (a scientist who studies the ocean) and the first woman to pilot the deep submergence vehicle *Alvin*. She spent 2 years taking other scientists to the bottom of the sea to study life there. A species of shrimp, *Chorocaris vandoverae*, has been named in her honor.

Idawally Zorada Lewis (1842-1911) was 15 years old when her family moved to Lime Rock Lighthouse in Newport, Rhode Island. After her father became ill, Ida took over his work tending the light and rowing to the mainland for supplies. During her 39 years at the lighthouse, she rescued more than a dozen men from drowning (turn to page 14 to see a painting of her in action).

Sharon Daley is a registered nurse who lives on an island off the coast of Maine. Twice a month she travels to other islands that have no doctors or hospitals and runs a floating health clinic. She operates teleconferencing equipment to allow mainland doctors to examine and treat their distant patients.

Terry-Ann Gregory of the U.S. Coast Guard was stationed out of Miami from 1998 to 2002. She became a recruiter in Washington, D.C., and then qualified for Officer Candidate School training at the Coast Guard Academy in New London, Connecticut. She is originally from the Island of Jamaica.

Hannah Snell (1723-1792) disguised herself as a man to join the British Navy in the 1740s. She spent 9 years at sea and earned a reputation for being a courageous sailor.

Kathleen McGrath (1952-2002) was the first woman to command a U.S. warship, the 453-foot-long frigate USS *Jarrett*. She once told a reporter, "I don't try to emulate a man, nor do I try to do what a guy would do. I have to be myself." Women made up 14 percent of the U.S. Navy in 2001.

Linda Greenlaw is well known as the Gloucester swordfishing captain who survived the "Perfect Storm" of 1991. She now works her own lobster boat at Isle au Haut, off the coast of Maine. She has written several best-selling books about her experiences at sea.

Catherine Via and **Beatrice Taylor** are sisters who own and operate a crab house on the Chesapeake Bay. Beatrice catches the crabs and Catherine sorts and packs them for shipping.

Mary Brewster (1822-1878) was one of the first captains' wives to go on a whaling voyage. In 1845, at age 23, she sailed with her husband William Brewster from Stonington, Connecticut. During her 6 years at sea, Mary visited Hawaii and became the first American woman to pass through the Bering Strait into the Arctic Ocean.

Susan Peterson Howell (1947-1984) was an experienced sailor and navigation instructor. In 1984, she was on the tall ship *Marques* near Bermuda when a storm hit and the ship sank, killing her and 18 other people aboard.

Mary K. Bercaw Edwards sailed around the world with her family when she was a teenager. She now teaches maritime literature to college students and demonstrates traditional sailor's skills to visitors at Mystic Seaport.

Mary Patten (1837-1861) was 19 years old when she joined her husband, a merchant ship captain, on a voyage from New York to California. When Capt. Patten fell ill, Mary was the only one aboard who knew how to navigate. She brought the ship safely around Cape Horn to San Francisco after 136 days at sea.

Electa "Exy" Johnson and her husband Irving sailed around the world 7 times in 30 years, training hundreds of young sailors aboard the *Yankee*, a tall ship and floating classroom.

Jennifer Irving captains the sail-training vessels of the Sea Education Association. During the past 15 years, she has never been ashore for more than three months at a time!

Jennifer L. Yount graduated from the U.S. Coast Guard Academy in 1991 and spent 8 years at sea, eventually commanding the cutter *Dauntless*. She now teaches at California Maritime Academy, the first school that admitted women into a licensed maritime program.

Mary "Ma" Greene (1874-1949) was a riverboat pilot and captain on the Mississippi River for more than 50 years. She lived aboard a steamboat with her husband Gordon (also a captain) and their 3 sons. Mary loved to talk and dance with the boat's passengers, who nicknamed her "Ma."

Thea Christiansen Foss was a Norwegian immigrant who lived in Tacoma, Washington, in the 1880s, and started renting out rowboats to support her family. When she died, her company owned more than 200 boats. Tacoma's Thea Foss Waterway was named in her honor.

Ellen McArthur, an Englishwoman, began sailing at age 8 with her aunt. In 2001, at age 24, she became the youngest woman to sail alone around the world, taking just 94 days to complete the voyage.

Michele Gladwin captains the 1,100-foot-long *Arnold Maersk*, one of the largest containerships in the world. Originally from Denmark, Gladwin now travels the oceans delivering goods to ports in Europe, Asia, and the United States. She was the first woman promoted to the rank of captain at Maersk, the world's biggest shipping company.

Credits

Page 6, ©Mystic Seaport, Rosenfeld Collection 15794F
Page 7, l: Courtesy of Dawn Riley, America True, San Francisco, California
Page 7, r: Courtesy of Dawn Riley, America True, San Francisco, California
Page 7, t: Mystic Seaport 1995.58.2
Page 8-9, Engraving from Charles Johnson, *A General History of the Robberies and Murders of the Most Notorious Pyrates* (London, 1724), courtesy of the New York Public Library
Page 10, Courtesy of Beinecke Rare Book and Manuscript Library, Yale University, 3613310
Page 11, t: Photograph by K. Sullivan, courtesy of Cindy Lee Van Dover
Page 11, b: Photograph by Richard J. King, 2004, basalt lava courtesy of Lisa Gilbert
Page 12, Daniel Maclise, *The Death of Nelson* (1864), courtesy of National Museums Liverpool
Page 13, l: "Miss Ida Lewis, The Heroine of Newport," *Harper's Weekly*, July 31, 1869
Page 13, b: "The Naval Hospital Red Rover," *Harper's Weekly*, May 9, 1863
Page 13, r: Photograph by Michael Johnson, courtesy of Sharon Daley, 2004
Page 14, John Witt, *Ida Lewis Makes a Rescue at Lime Rock*, courtesy of the United States Coast Guard
Page 15, l: Courtesy of The Mariners' Museum
Page 15, m: Courtesy of the United States Coast Guard, 1999, 990616-C-7777A-502
Page 15, r: Photograph by PA1 Carolyn Cihelka, courtesy of the United States Coast Guard, 1992, 920301-C-0930C-002
Page 16, Engraved portrait of Hannah Snell, originally published in *The Female Soldier, or The Surprising Life and Adventures of Hannah Snell* (London, 1750), as reproduced in Menie Muriel Dowie, ed., *Women Adventurers* (London: T.F. Unwin, 1893), collection of the Boston Athenaeum
Page 17, l: Figurehead, Mystic Seaport 1953.3098
Page 17, m: Courtesy of The Mariners' Museum
Page 17, r: Photograph by Ed Kashi with permission from Gregory Brandon
Page 18, William Sydney Mount, *Eel Spearing at Setauket* (1845), courtesy of the New York State Historical Association
Page 19, l: Photograph by Tom Ring, courtesy of Linda Greenlaw
Page 19, t: T-shirt courtesy of Linda Greenlaw
Page 19, r: Photograph by Starke Jett, courtesy of The Mariners' Museum
Page 20, Daguerreotype by J. Gurnsey, ca. 1854, Mystic Seaport, 1948.1146
Page 21, l: Photograph by George E. Hall, Mystic Seaport 84-6-66
Page 21, r: Photograph by Richard J. King, 2004
Page 22-23, Gordon Johnson, *Mary Patten on the Deck of Neptune's Car*, courtesy of the Atlantic Mutual Insurance Company
Page 24, "Girl Scouts Learn to Sail Aboard the *Liberty*," ca. 1930s, photograph courtesy of The Mariners' Museum
Page 25, l: Photograph by Lee Uran, 2003, www.Brigantines.com
Page 25, m: Courtesy of California Maritime Academy, 2004
Page 25, r: Photograph by Shannon McCarthy, 2003
Page 26, l: Photograph courtesy of The Mariners' Museum
Page 26, r: Photograph, ca. 1910, courtesy of Foss Maritime Company
Page 27, l: Photograph by Phil Russel, 2000, with permission of PPL Ltd.
Page 27, r: Photograph by Ann Nissen, 2000

In addition to the inspiring women featured, an extraordinary number of people went into the production of this book, providing images, design, ideas, research, and support. These people include, but are definitely not limited to: Linda Cusano (designer), Karen Belmore, John Jensen, Peggy Tate Smith, Louisa Watrous, Amy German, Dennis Murphy, Christopher Freeman, Andy German, Jonathan Shay, Arleen Andersen, Susan Funk, Wendy Schnur, Jennifer Whitty, Sara Harris, Nathan Adams, Britta Granrud, David S. Howell, Gregory Brandon, Hart Kelley, and Lisa and Bingo Gilbert. And special thank you to The Mariners' Museum.

Mystic Seaport
75 Greenmanville Avenue
PO Box 6000
Mystic, CT 06355-0990

ISBN 0-939511-07-x